I'm Going To

These levels are meant only as guides;
you and your child can best choose a book that's right.

Level 1: Kindergarten–Grade 1 . . . Ages 4–6
- word bank to highlight new words
- consistent placement of text to promote readability
- easy words and phrases
- simple sentences build to make simple stories
- art and design help new readers decode text

Level 2: Grade 1 . . . Ages 6–7
- word bank to highlight new words
- rhyming texts introduced
- more difficult words, but vocabulary is still limited
- longer sentences and longer stories
- designed for easy readability

Level 3: Grade 2 . . . Ages 7–8
- richer vocabulary of up to 200 different words
- varied sentence structure
- high-interest stories with longer plots
- designed to promote independent reading

Level 4: Grades 3 and up . . . Ages 8 and up
- richer vocabulary of more than 300 different words
- short chapters, multiple stories, or poems
- more complex plots for the newly independent reader
- emphasis on reading for meaning

LEVEL 3

2 4 6 8 10 9 7 5 3 1

Published by Sterling Publishing Co., Inc.
387 Park Avenue South, New York, NY 10016
Text © 2007 by Arlene Neveloff
Illustrations © 2007 by Emily Bolam
Distributed in Canada by Sterling Publishing
c/o Canadian Manda Group, 165 Dufferin Street
Toronto, Ontario, Canada M6K 3H6
Distributed in the United Kingdom by GMC Distribution Services,
Castle Place, 166 High Street, Lewes, East Sussex, England BN7 1XU
Distributed in Australia by Capricorn Link (Australia) Pty. Ltd.
P.O. Box 704, Windsor, NSW 2756, Australia

I'm Going To Read is a trademark of Sterling Publishing Co., Inc.

Library of Congress Cataloging-in-Publication Data

Neveloff, Arlene.
  Jackson finds a home / written by Arlene Neveloff ; pictures by Emily Bolam.
    p. cm.—(I'm going to read)
  Summary: Jackson, a big brown dog, lives at an animal shelter and dearly
wants to be adopted.
  ISBN-13: 978-1-4027-3078-8
  ISBN-10: 1-4027-3078-0
  [1. Dogs—Fiction. 2. Animal shelters—Fiction. 3. Adoption—Fiction.] I. Bolam,
Emily, ill. II. Title.

PZ7.B635848Jac 2007
[E]—dc22

                                                        2006101110

Sterling ISBN-13: 978-1-4027-3078-8
Sterling ISBN-10: 1-4027-3078-0

For information about custom editions, special sales, premium and
corporate purchases, please contact Sterling Special Sales
Department at 800-805-5489 or specialsales@sterlingpub.com.

Jackson
Finds a Home

Story by Arlene Neveloff
Pictures by Emily Bolam

STERLING

Jackson is a BIG brown dog.
He lives in an animal shelter.

A man with a purple sweater visits Jackson.
He takes him for a walk.
Maybe he will adopt Jackson.

Jackson chases a gray squirrel.
The man chases the squirrel too!

"I need a pet that can sit still.
This dog is too wild,"
he says.

The man will not
take Jackson home.

A lady with a red coat takes Jackson for a walk. Maybe she will adopt him.

Jackson runs through a puddle.
Splash, splash, splat!

Jackson is very muddy.
The lady is very wet.

"I need a clean pet.
This dog is too messy,"
she says.

The lady will not
take Jackson home.

Another man takes Jackson for a walk.
Maybe he will adopt Jackson.

Jackson barks
at another dog.
He barks and barks.

BARK!
BARK!

BARK!
BARK!
BARK!

"This dog is not for me," he says.
"He is too noisy!
I need a quiet pet."

Sam and Sara visit the shelter.
They are happy to take
Jackson for a walk.

Jackson jumps into a deep pile
of wet leaves.
Sam and Sara jump in too.

Jackson rolls in the leaves.
The kids throw leaves in the air.

They laugh, "We like to
get wet . . . and dirty!"

Jackson sees a squirrel.
He begins to run.

Sam and Sara run
           after Jackson . . .

. . . until they catch him!

Jackson jumps on them.
He gives them wet and sloppy kisses.

Sam pats his nose.
Sara scratches behind his ears.

"Would you like to go home
with us?" they ask.

secret treats . . .

and belly rubs.

Sam and Sara adopt Jackson.

Jackson adopts Sam and Sara!